The Minestrone Mob

written by Karen Wallace
illustrated by Judy Brown

PiCTURE WiNDOW BOOKS
Minneapolis, Minnesota

Editor: Nick Healy
Page Production: Brandie E. Shoemaker
Creative Director: Keith Griffin
Editorial Director: Carol Jones

First American edition published in 2007 by
Picture Window Books
5115 Excelsior Boulevard
Suite 232
Minneapolis, MN 55416
877-845-8392
www.picturewindowbooks.com

First published in 1999 by A&C Black Publishers Limited, 38 Soho Square,
London W1D 3HB, with the title THE MINESTRONE MOB.

Text copyright © Karen Wallace 1999
Illustrations copyright © Judy Brown 1999

Printed in the United States of America.

Library of Congress Cataloging-in-Publication Data
Wallace, Karen.
The Minestrone Mob / by Karen Wallace & Judy Brown.— 1st American ed.
p. cm. — (Read-it! chapter books)
Summary: Lettuce Leef and Nimble Charlie, the Crook Catchers to the
Queen, investigate the disappearance of the queen's recipe for minestrone
soup—as well as her clothing.
ISBN-13: 978-1-4048-2723-3 (hardcover)
ISBN-10: 1-4048-2723-4 (hardcover)
[1. Robbers and outlaws—Fiction. 2. Kings, queens, rulers, etc.—Fiction. 3.
Mystery and detective stories.] I. Brown, Judy, 1962– ill. II. Title. III. Series.
PZ7.W1568Min 2007
[E]—dc22   2006003379

Table of Contents

Chapter One

Lettuce Leef and Nimble Charlie were the queen's Crook Catchers.

Their office was hidden inside a giant pumpkin and connected to the palace by an emergency telephone.

Now it was ringing!

"Sounds like an emergency to me,"
Nimble Charlie said.

Lettuce Leef headed for the door.

Crook Catchers
to the rescue!

The palace door opened before the Crook Catchers even had time to knock. Lettuce Leef gasped.

Splatter, the queen's trusty servant, stood there in his pajamas.

"What happened to your uniform?" asked Nimble Charlie, trying not to stare.

Lettuce Leef hid a smile. Splatter's top was covered with blue bunnies.

"Splatter!" bellowed the queen from inside the palace.

Chapter Two

The queen's room was a terrible
mess. Cooking books and bits of
paper covered the floor.

Most extraordinary of all, the queen
was standing in the middle of the
room in her pajamas.

Lettuce Leef
bowed, so she
didn't have
to look.

Nimble Charlie
quickly curtsied
by mistake.

Splatter quickly held out the
queen's bathrobe.

"Your Majesty," said Nimble Charlie gently, "what's going on?"

It's a disaster! We've lost our minestrone recipe! Prince Linguini will abandon us!

"Who's Prince Linguini?" asked Lettuce Leef. "And why aren't you wearing your normal clothes?"

"They were stolen," muttered Splatter. The queen held up a copy of the *Daily Screamer*.

Lettuce Leef and Nimble Charlie exchanged looks. What was going on?

"The queen and Prince Linguini are swapping royal gifts today," explained Splatter. "A truckload of his famous Spaghetti Hoops for 50 barrels of her homemade minestrone soup!"

Nimble Charlie thought hard. The stolen clothes and the stolen recipe had to be connected.

Splatter blushed and twirled a piece
of hair in his fingers.

"What did they want from you?"
asked Nimble Charlie.

"They said they were tourists,"
mumbled Splatter.

They asked if they could look around.

"I hope you told them to get lost,"
bellowed the queen.

Splatter swallowed hard.

The queen took a step toward him.

Splatter opened his mouth, but the only thing that came out was a small, strangled squeak.

Chapter Three

The queen's face was almost
touching Splatter's nose.

Suddenly, a tube of tomato paste
whizzed through the open window.

It had a note tied to it.

Tough noodles, Queenie.
We got your clothes, and
we got the prince.
And we'll get your Hoops.
Too bad you can't join us
for supper.
Signed, Redbits and Sludge,
The Minestrone Mob.

The queen stomped her foot and made a rude noise.

If these people think they can fool the prince by dressing up in our clothes, they're out of their tiny minds!

Why's that?

At that moment, another tube of
tomato paste whizzed through
the window.

A pair of crushed eyeglasses was tied
to it.

Nobody spoke. Splatter began
to shake. "I forgot to tell you,"
he whispered.

I found this in
the laundry room.

He handed Lettuce Leef a folded
card. She read it aloud.

The Minestrone Mob
Wannabe Movie Moguls
but Mostly Thieves

All payments in spaghetti.
Prince Linguini's Spaghetti Hoops preferred.

The queen stared at Splatter and
went red with rage.

Lettuce Leef and Nimble Charlie ran
to the door.

Chapter Four

Back in their pumpkin office, Lettuce Leef and Nimble Charlie looked at the clues.

"Where would you go if you were planning to trick the prince into thinking he was having soup with a queen?" asked Lettuce Leef.

Nimble Charlie thought hard.

Lettuce Leef looked at the calling card. "Wannabe Movie Moguls," she muttered.

All afternoon, Lettuce Leef and
Nimble Charlie looked at movie sets.

But they didn't see a fake banquet hall in a fake palace anywhere.

"Maybe I was wrong," said Nimble Charlie as they turned down a fake tree-lined avenue.

"Maybe not!" Lettuce Leef pointed to a huge cardboard-looking castle at the end of the avenue. In front of it was an enormous truck.

Nimble Charlie peered through his extra-strong binoculars. A picture of a prince eating Spaghetti Hoops was painted on the side of the truck.

"Bull's-eye!" cried Nimble Charlie.

Lettuce Leef called the queen and made a plan.

Chapter Five

Inside the fake banquet hall, Redbits was getting nervous. Dressing up as the queen was all fine and well, but talking to Prince Linguini was another thing.

"Are you feeling well, Your Majesty?" asked Prince Linguini. He felt his way around the banquet table. Without his glasses, he couldn't see a thing.

Redbits jammed his crown halfway
down his head.

Prince Linguini pursed his lips.
Perhaps the queen had seen too
many cops-and-robbers movies. "As
you wish, Your Majesty," he replied.

In front of Prince Linguini, the
knives and forks and china were
a blur. He found what he was
looking for and tied his napkin
around his neck.

In the kitchen of the cardboard palace, Sludge stirred a huge pot of the queen's minestrone.

He slurped a spoonful. It tasted really delicious. But nothing, absolutely nothing in the world, was as delicious as Prince Linguini's Spaghetti Hoops.

Sludge's stomach rumbled, and his hand trembled. Any minute now, a lifetime supply of Spaghetti Hoops would be his. He peeped into the hall.

Redbits and Prince Linguini were ready to make the trade.

Sludge slipped into Splatter's uniform and picked up the pot of minestrone soup.

Suddenly, Nimble Charlie jumped out from his hiding place. He whipped a thick black sack over Sludge's head.

WHOOMPH!

A few seconds later, the real Splatter
picked up the huge soup pot and
headed for the banquet hall.

Chapter Six

Underneath the banquet table, Lettuce Leef explained her plan to the queen.

That was a tricky question. Aside
from Redbits' voice and the stubble
on his chin, there was not a lot
of difference between him and
the queen.

At that moment, a marvelous and mouthwatering smell wafted through the air. It was the queen's minestrone.

"The soup awaits, Your Majesty," said the real Splatter.

There was no time to lose. Lettuce
Leef and the queen crawled to the
end of the table.

Redbits' dirty sneakers poked out
from under the queen's best gown.

Lettuce Leef swiftly untied the laces
and silently tied them around the
chair legs.

There was a clatter of spoons and
bowls above.

Soup is
served.

Before Redbits had time to pick up
his spoon ...

WHOOMPH!

... Nimble Charlie jumped from his
hiding place and whipped a black
sack over Redbits' head. Then he
tipped back the chair and dragged
Redbits away.

In the same moment, Lettuce Leef grabbed another chair. "Go," she whispered to the queen.

Quick as a flash, the queen threw herself into the new chair. Luckily, Prince Linguini was so busy slurping his soup that he didn't notice a thing.

Just then, Splatter dragged Redbits and Sludge into the room.

The queen poked Redbits in the stomach. "If they can make one pot of my own minestrone, they can make 50 barrels for Prince Linguini!" she said.

She banged her fist on the table.

The queen jumped onto the table.

Look for More
Read-it!
Chapter Books

Looking for a specific title? A complete list
of *Read-it!* Chapter Books is available on our Web site:
www.picturewindowbooks.com